FANTASTIC BEASTS
AND WHERE
TO FIND THEM™

MAGICAL CREATURES
COLORING BOOK

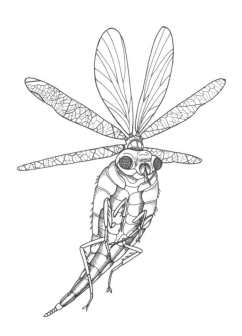

HarperCollins books may be purchased for educational, business, or sales promotional use. For information please email the Special Markets Department at SPsales@harpercollins.com.

Published in 2016 by
Harper Design
An Imprint of HarperCollins*Publishers*
195 Broadway
New York, NY 10007
Tel: (212) 207-7000
Fax: (855) 746-6023

Distributed throughout North America by
HarperCollins Publishers
195 Broadway
New York, NY 10007

ISBN 978-0-06-257134-2

Printed and bound in USA

Illustrations by Nicolette Caven (5, 10–11, 14, 17, 20, 25, 26–7, 29, 30–1, 35, 36, 38–9, 43, 48–9, 53, 54, 66–7, 70–1, 72, 80), Micaela Alcaino (6–7, 15, 21, 24, 28, 46, 50–1, 52, 59, 60–1, 62, 63, 74–5) & Mike Topping (12–13, 16, 18–19, 22, 32–3, 42, 44–5, 47, 57, 58, 64, 68–9, 74–5, 76–7)

Project Editor: Chris Smith
Cover design: Simeon Greenaway
Production Manager: Kathy Turtle

HarperCollins would like to thank Victoria Selover, Elaine Piechowski, Melanie Swartz & Jill Benscoter.

FANTASTIC BEASTS
AND WHERE TO FIND THEM™

MAGICAL CREATURES
COLORING BOOK

HARPER DESIGN
An Imprint of HarperCollins Publishers

When Newt Scamander sets off on his travels around the world to track and document fantastic beasts, their existence is largely unknown to Muggles and No-Majs, thanks to Clause 73 of the International Statute of Wizarding Secrecy. Even within the wizarding world few are aware there are so *many*.

That nearly changes when the English wizard arrives in New York with a battered leather case. The seemingly ordinary looking item is home and refuge to a magical menagerie of beasts, looked after by Newt as he expands his knowledge of Magizoology. But not all are content to stay inside...

From the Niffler, Erumpent, and Murtlap to the Demiguise, Occamy, and Thunderbird, their color and appearance is as fantastic as their habitats located inside Newt's case. Many more are hidden there, including such beasts as the pink-plumed Fwooper, the vivid blue Billywig, the sprig-like, tree-dwelling Bowtruckle, and the brown, fairy-like Doxy.

Turn the page and continue coloring your way into the wizarding world, as you join Newt and his friends Jacob, Tina, and Queenie on their quest through New York – from its streets, subway, and zoo to MACUSA's magical headquarters – to find the fantastic beasts!

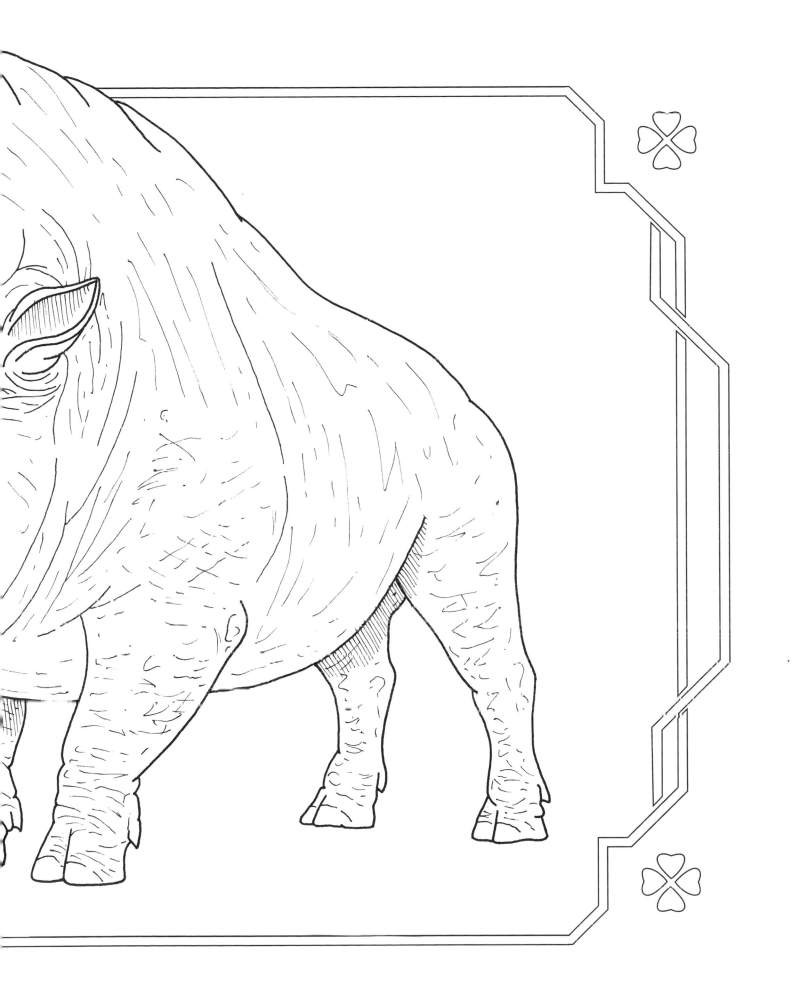

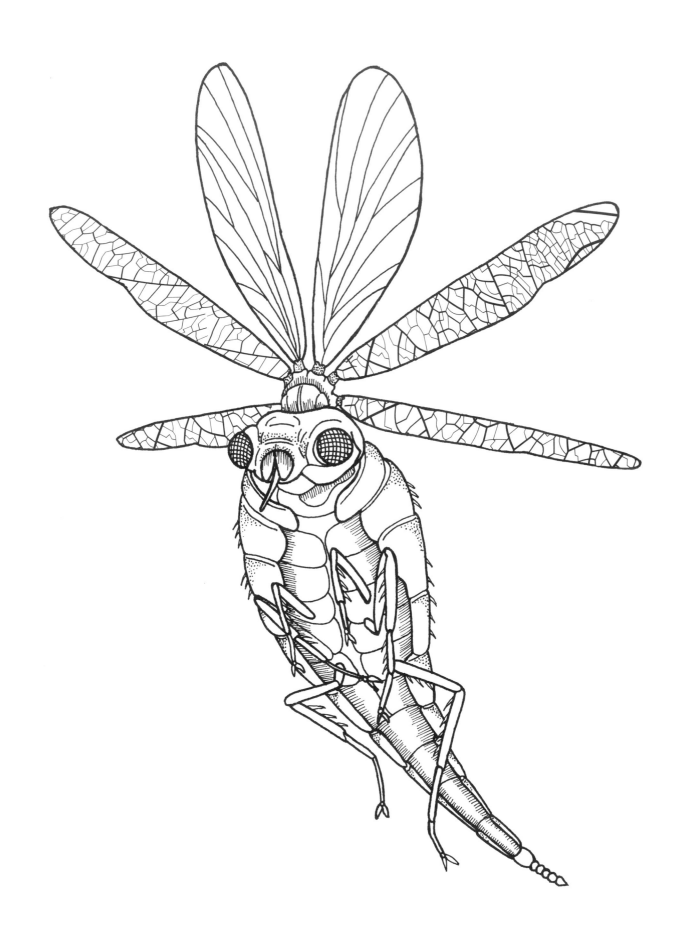

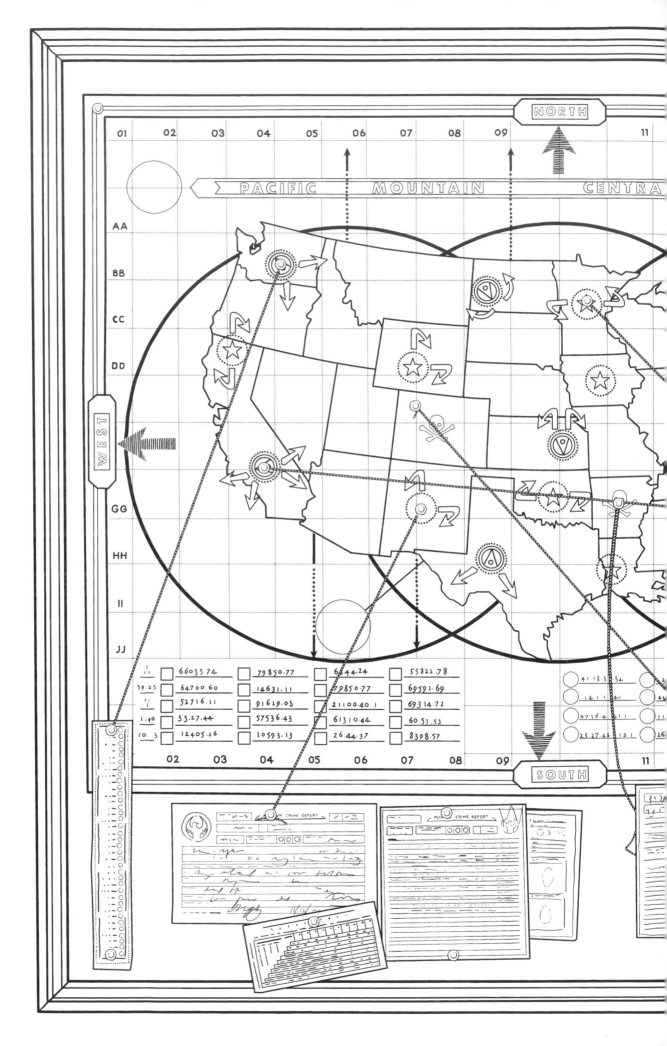

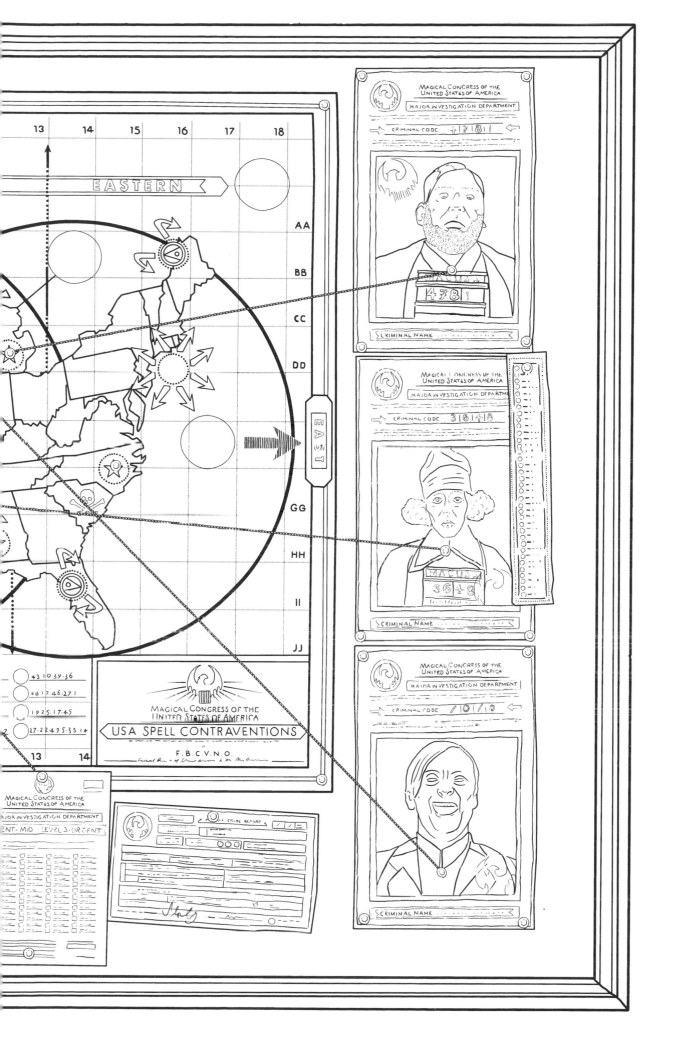

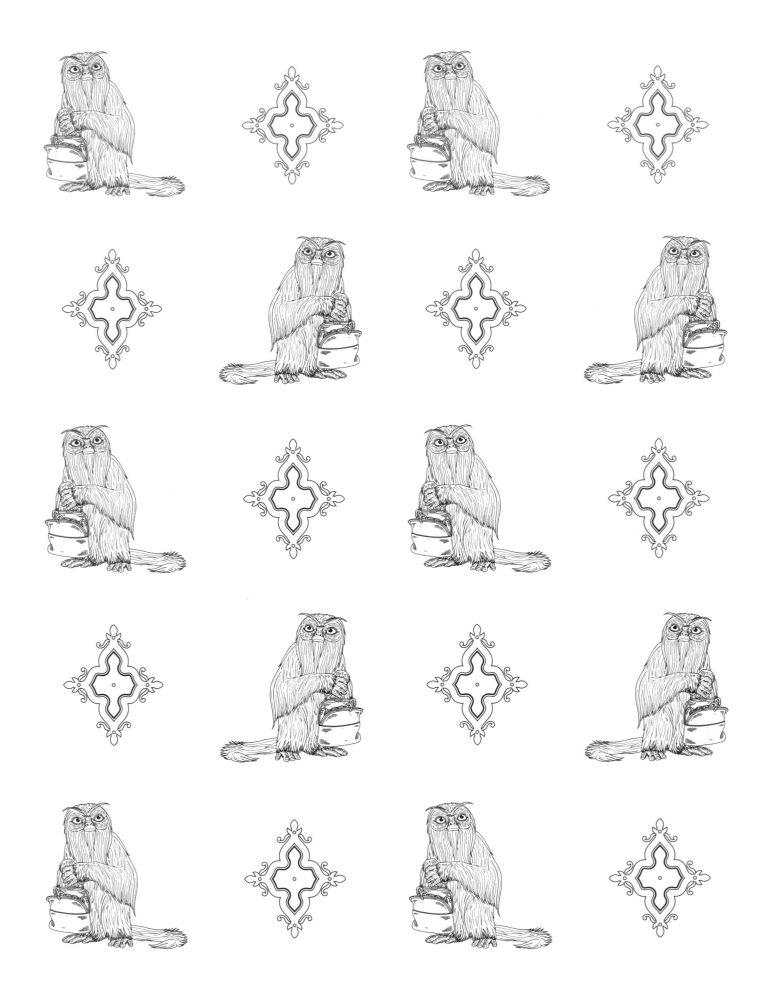

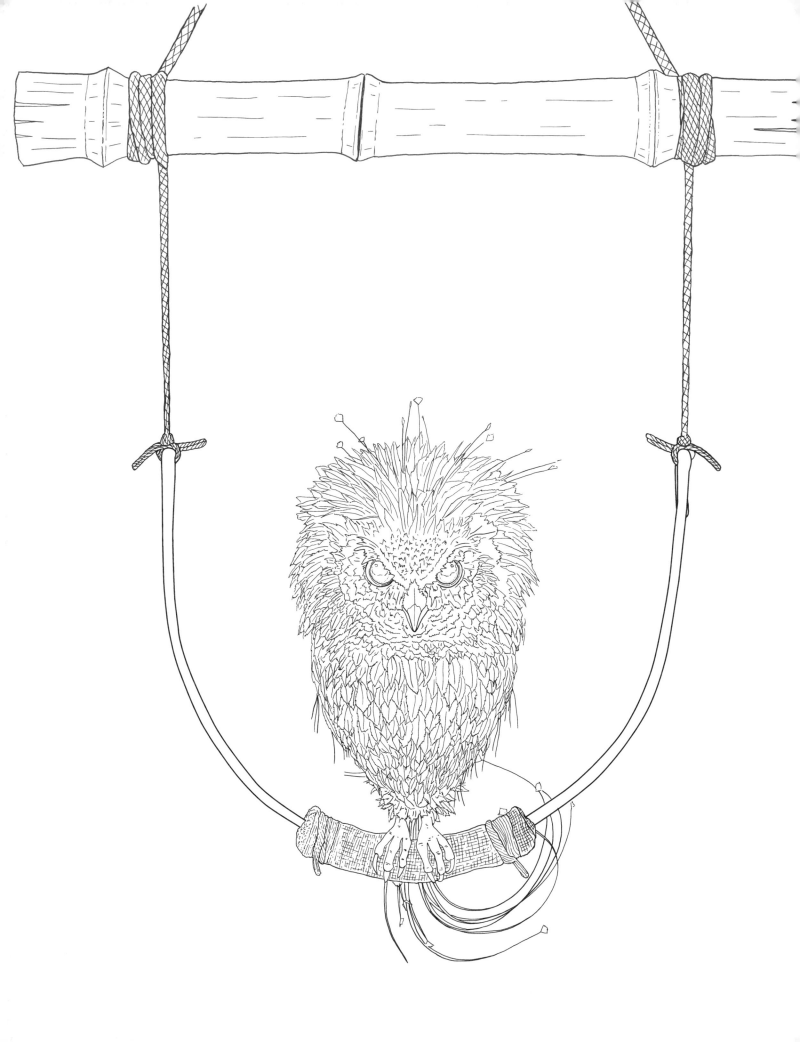

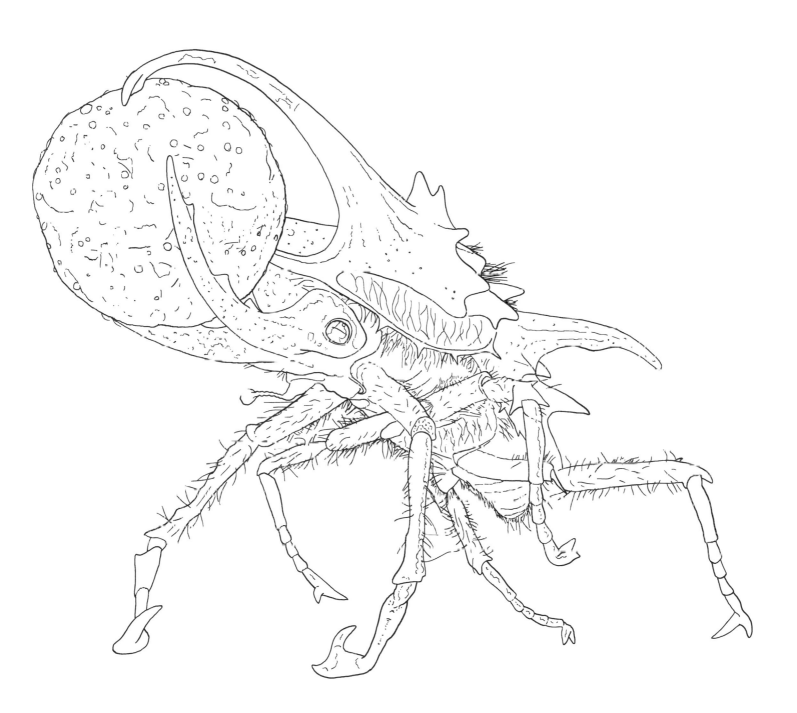

MINISTRATION CHART
To Assist Magical Creature Welfare and Development

39423

42339

№ 289295

HABITAT & TERRAIN CODES

⊕	Aquatic / Amphibious
▲	Burrowing
⋎	Desert
✦	Tropical/Equatorial
◈	Temperate

A Guide to the Classification of
ALL KNOWN BEASTS, BEINGS & SPIRITS.

XXXXX	KNOWN WIZARD KILLER IMPOSSIBLE TO TRAIN OR DOMESTICATE
XXXX	DANGEROUS REQUIRES SPECIALIST KNOWLEDGE SKILLED WIZARD MAY HANDLE
XXX	COMPETENT WIZARD SHOULD COPE
XX	HARMLESS MAY BE DOMESTICATED
X	BORING

MINISTRY OF MAGIC
(M.o.M.) LONDON

SPECIAL FEED CODES

🦅	Beaked (excl. Griffin)
🪶	Feathered
🦌	Horned
🐾	Hooved (not Nogtails)
🐚	Carapaced

DEPT. FOR THE REGULATION AND CONTROL OF MAGICAL CREATURES

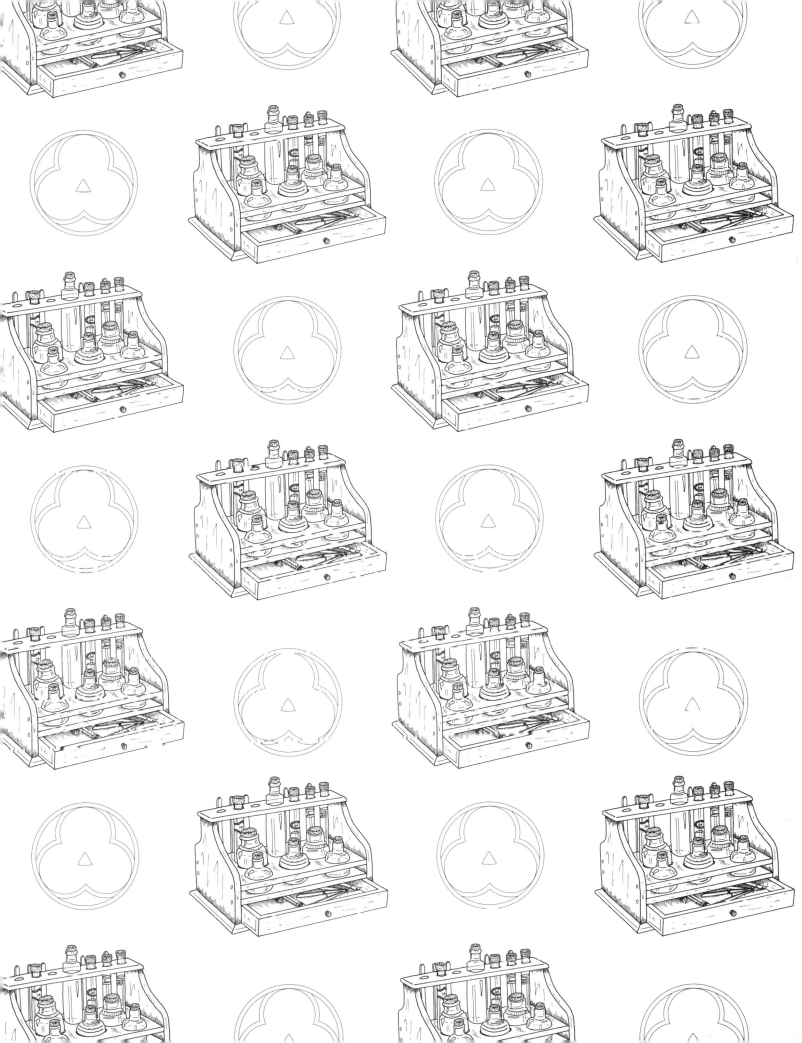

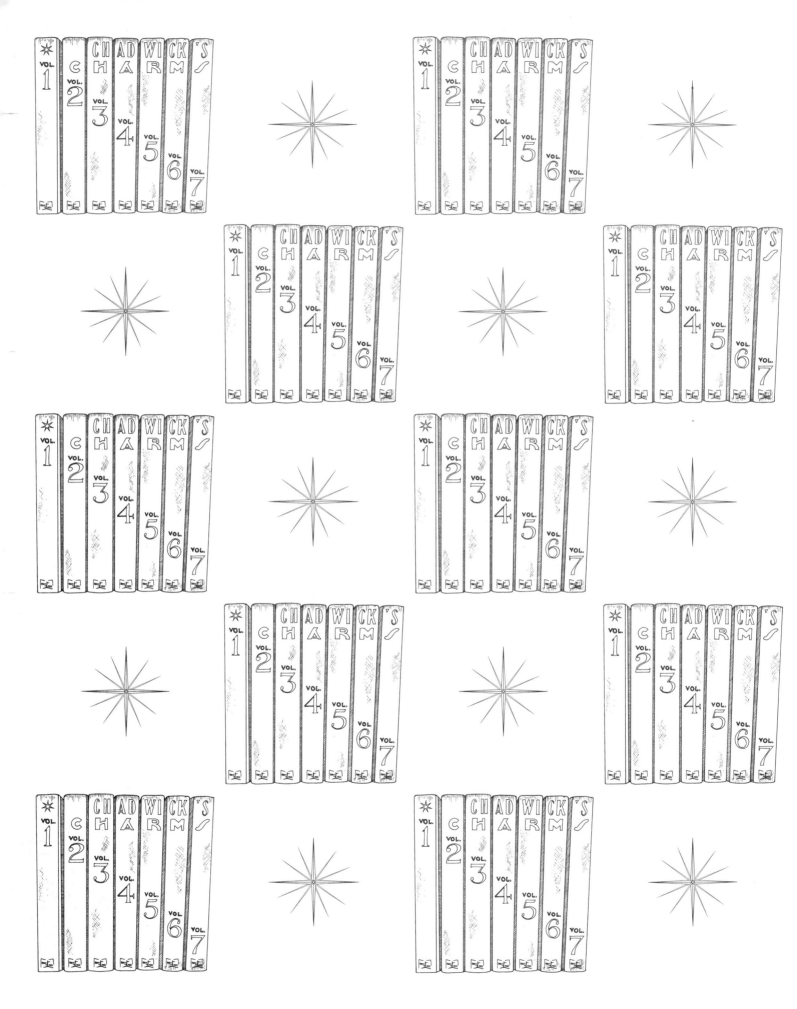

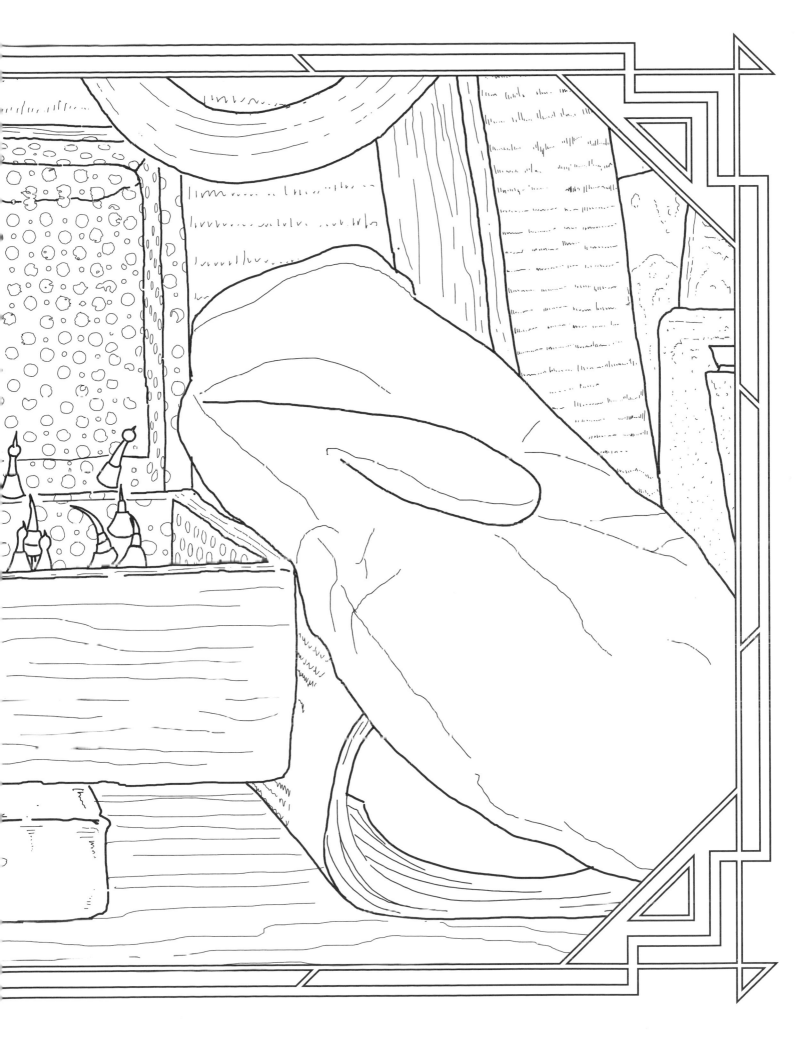

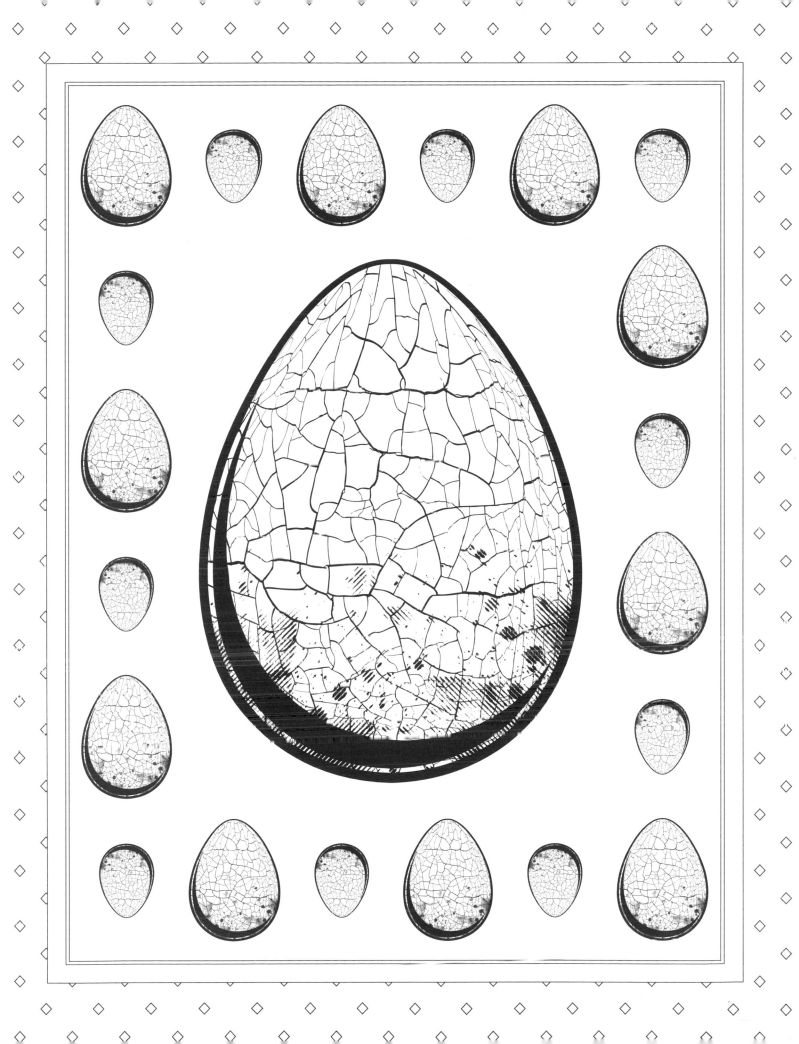